Superfairies

The Snow Fairy

by Janey Louise Jones
illustrated by Jennie Poh

PICTURE WINDOW BOOKS
a capstone imprint

Superfairies is published by Picture Window Books
A Capstone Imprint
1710 Roe Crest Drive
North Mankato, Minnesota 56003
www.mycapstone.com

Library of Congress Cataloging-in-Publication Data
Names: Jones, Janey, 1968- author. | Poh, Jennie, illustrator.
Title: The Snow Fairy / by Janey Louise Jones; [illustrator,
Jennie Poh].
Description: North Mankato, Minnesota : Picture Window
  Books, a Capstone imprint, [2018] | Series: Superfairies |
  Summary: It is time for the winter Sparkle Ball, so
  when Billy the badger has the Snow Fairy's crown
  snatched from his paws by a greedy magpie, who loves
  sparkly things, it is up to the Superfairies to retrieve it
  and save the Ball. |
Identifiers: LCCN 2017039779 (print) | LCCN
  2017042130 (ebook) | ISBN 9781515824268 (eBook
  PDF) | ISBN 9781515824244 (hardcover) | ISBN
  9781515824282 (pbk.)
Subjects: LCSH: Fairies—Juvenile fiction. | Crowns—
  Juvenile fiction. | Animals—Juvenile fiction. | CYAC:
  Fairies—Fiction. | Balls (Parties)—Fiction. | Crowns—
  Fiction. | Forest animals—Fiction.
Classification: LCC PZ7.J72019 (ebook) | LCC PZ7.J72019
  Sn 2018 (print) | DDC [E]--dc23
LC record available at https://lccn.loc.gov/2017039779

Designer: Tracy McCabe

Printed and bound in the United States of America.
011008R

Table of Contents

The Fairy World

The Superfairies of Peaseblossom Woods use
teamwork to rescue animals in trouble. They
bring together their special superskills,
petal power, and lots of love.

Superfairy Rose

can blow super healing fairy
kisses to make the animals in
Peaseblossom Woods feel better.

Superfairy Berry

can see for miles
around with her
super eyesight.

Superfairy Star

can create super dazzling
brightness in one dainty spin
to lighten up dark places.

Superfairy Silk

spins super strong webs
for animal rescues.

Chapter 1

Snowy Day

It was a snowy day in Peaseblossom
Woods, and everyone was getting ready
for the Snow Fairy's Sparkle Ball. The ball
only came around once a year, but it was
well worth the wait.

Lacy snowflakes tumbled from the sky
and landed silently on the snowy ground.
Icicles hung from tree branches like
delicate crystal jewelry. Inside the cherry
blossom tree, the Superfairies were
admiring the pretty winter landscape.

"Everything looks so beautiful in a
blizzard!" exclaimed Star, looking out
of the window of the cozy living room.

"I love snowflakes. Is it true that every single one is different?"

"Yes!" said Berry. "That's true. But when they melt, they all turn to water just the same!"

"I don't want the snow to melt!" said Silk, twirling. "I wish it could be winter forever!"

"But wouldn't you miss the spring flowers?" Rose asked. "And the summer sun? And the autumn colors?"

"Maybe just a tiny bit," admitted Silk. "But isn't it lovely being all snuggled up in our sweet little house with the fire and lanterns and delicious food?"

"It definitely is!" said Rose. She fluttered over and warmed her hands in front of the crackling fire.

"I hope we can make it through all this snow to Icy Hollow for the Sparkle Ball," said Star.

"Me too!" said Berry. "I can't wait to see if the Snow Fairy likes the winter crown we've made for her this year." She attached some more berries and crystals to the wonderful, delicate crown she'd made. It dazzled on the dining table.

"That looks just beautiful!" Rose exclaimed. "Well done, Berry! I love it!"

"Thanks, but it isn't just my work," said Berry. "We've all worked hard on the crown. I think the Snow Fairy will love it too!"

"Let's try on our gowns for the ball now!" suggested Silk.

"Yipppee!" cried Star. "I just adore dressing up!"

"Remember we don't have long until we have to leave!" said Rose.

"Hurry then! I want to see how we look!" said Star.

In the woods, the snow was coming down. It covered the ground like thick frosting on a cake. It was almost too cold to play outdoors. Even so, the animals were very excited about the Sparkle Ball.

Over at Copperwood Stables, the ponies were almost ready to leave.

"It's time to gather everyone for the ball!" said Dancer the Wild Pony. "Are you ready, Cloud?"

"Yes! I just hope that our feet don't freeze in the deep snow!" Cloud replied.

"It's not too far," said Dancer. "If we run, we will hardly notice the cold. Let's go!"

Dancer and Cloud set off through the woods. They pulled a pretty painted caravan behind them to collect their woodland friends. They lifted their dainty feet through the thick snow, kicking up little flurries of soft snow as they went.

"Are your feet really cold?" Dancer asked.

"Not as bad as I feared. I'm just so excited!" said Cloud. "I can't wait!"

At the big oak tree, the rest of the animals waited in a huddle for Cloud and Dancer to arrive. Violet the Velvet Rabbit and Susie Squirrel couldn't stop chattering about what the Snow Fairy's gown would look like.

"I think it will be as white as fresh snow and very elegant!" said Violet.

"Maybe it will be embroidered with snowflake designs!" exclaimed Susie.

Sonny Squirrel and Basil the Bear Cub were also looking forward to the ball.

"I can't wait to slide along the icy dance floor," said Sonny.

"And chase each other!" Basil agreed.

Billy Badger and Martha Mouse were most excited for the feast. It was a famous feast, and the little animals had never been to it before. But they had heard all about it from older relatives.

"There will be warm herb bread with creamy butter and lots of fruit pies!" said Billy. "Yum!"

"I am hoping for iced fairy cakes," Martha said. "And piles of ginger-cream cookies too! I love those!"

Just then, Dancer and Cloud arrived at the big oak tree. The animals were thrilled to see them. They piled into the caravan, chattering and giggling as they did so.

The journey to Icy Hollow was hard work for the dainty ponies. Thankfully, with all the animals singing cheerful winter songs, the time passed quickly.

They sang merrily:

"Crackling flames,
Winter games.
Toast your toes,
Warm your nose.
Hug your friend,
Warm cheer to send!"

"We're here!" cried Cloud as Icy
Hollow came into view. "At last!"

Chapter 2

Arrival at Icy Hollow

The animals hopped out of the caravan and looked around at Icy Hollow with wonder.

"It's dazzling!" said Susie.

"The icicles look like diamonds!" Martha exclaimed.

"It's an ice palace!" said Violet.

"Oooh, look! Here come the Superfairies in the Fairycopter!" said Martha. "I bet they'll look so beautiful."

The door of the Fairycopter burst open, and the Superfairies fluttered out. Rose carried the box holding the winter crown for the Snow Fairy.

"I hope the crown for the Snow Fairy is in that box! Is it true that it will light up if snow falls on it?" said Susie.

"Of course it won't!" tutted Sonny. "You say such silly things, Susie! Really!"

"We just saw the Snow Fairy!" Star called to the animals. "She's circling the sky above Icy Hollow to welcome us all."

Violet, Martha, and Susie held hands and looked to the sky with wonder.

"I can't wait to see her!" Violet exclaimed.

"There she is!" cried Susie. She gasped as the Snow Fairy came into view. "Oh, the gown is even lovelier than I imagined it would be."

The Snow Fairy floated down to join the animals, smiling widely to show pearly white teeth. Four snowy owls flapped around her as she flew, protecting her.

The Snow Fairy's white cloak was trimmed with fluffy down feathers, and she wore feather-lined boots of ivory velvet. Her golden hair fell in waves down her back, and her hair was covered with snowdrops. Her lips were of deepest red and her cheeks of palest pink, flushed by the cold air. On her hands she wore a warm velvet muff.

Once the Snow Fairy was seated on her throne, the snowy owls perched near her. Then the Sparkle Ball officially began!

Rose placed the crown in its box behind the throne. It would stay safely there until the ceremony to crown the Snow Fairy as Winter Queen.

The band struck up a tune. Dancer and Cloud danced with Violet and Susie.

But Sonny, Billy, and Basil didn't much enjoy dancing.

"It's going to be *ages* until the feast," complained Billy. "What shall we do first?"

"My mom said I have to be really good," said Basil, "otherwise I'm not going to be allowed to go to any special events *ever* again!"

"Same here," said Sonny. "Dad said he'll be so embarrassed if I'm naughty! I have promised to be good."

Billy looked behind the throne at the box containing the Snow Fairy's crown. He lifted the lid. It seemed to be winking at him.

It dazzled!

It twinkled!

It sparkled!

"Sonny," Billy whispered, "should we take the crown outside for a moment?

We can find out if it really *does* light up
in the snow. . . ."

"Oh, that would be great fun! But
we shouldn't really take it, should we?"
said Sonny, thinking about his promise
to his dad.

"We're not going to take it, just *borrow*
it," said Billy. "We can put it back before
anyone notices. No one will even miss it.
Don't be boring! Don't you want to see
if it lights up?"

Sonny grinned. He thought it was a brilliant idea. He was very curious to see if the crown would light up. But he was very scared of being caught and getting into trouble.

Billy didn't wait for his friends to reply. He padded over to the box and lifted the crown from it. Before anyone could stop him, he ran out into the woods at top speed.

Sonny and Basil followed behind.

Outside, Billy held the crown up to the falling snow.

"Oh, wow! Look, it's lighting —"

But before Billy could finish what he was saying, a greedy magpie swooped down and . . .

SNATCH!

The bird grabbed the crown out of Billy's hands and carried it up into the snowy skies.

"Oh, no!" said Billy. "What are we going to do?"

"We must get the Superfairies to help us!" said Basil. "Otherwise the Sparkle Ball will be ruined!"

Chapter 3

Superfairies to the Rescue!

Inside the Sparkle Ball, the Superfairies heard bells ringing.

Ting-aling-aling!

"That's strange!" said Star to Rose. "We've never had to do a rescue at the ball before!"

"There must be a good reason if the bells are ringing," Rose replied.

Berry and Silk joined Star and Rose at once.

"Ready to rescue!" called Rose. All the Superfairies headed outside and huddled around the Strawberry computer, which Rose carried in her bag at all times.

"What can you see, Rose?" asked Silk.

"Billy, Basil, and Sonny are not far from here. There's a magpie too," said Rose. "Oh, no! Look at the screen! The magpie has the Snow Fairy's crown! How could that have happened?"

The three boys joined the Superfairies. Billy was embarrassed.

"I'm really sorry," he said. "This is all my fault."

"What happened, Billy?" asked Rose. "How did the crown get outside?"

"We were just examining the crown for a minute," Billy said. "I wanted to see if it would light up. We were going to put it right back where we found it. But then the magpie flew down and took it right out of my hands."

"It was so quick!" Basil added, sounding flustered. "We didn't have time to do anything about it!"

"Did you see which way the magpie went?" asked Berry.

"That way!" said Sonny, pointing deep into the woods. The other two boys nodded in agreement.

"We must find the crown," said Rose anxiously. "Otherwise how can we crown the Snow Fairy as the Winter Queen?"

Billy felt very sorry and upset. Sonny and Basil were worried too — especially about what their moms and dads would say if they found out.

The Superfairies swooped into action, chasing after the naughty magpie.

"Come on," said Berry, using her bright eyes. "I can see the crown twinkling up ahead."

The magpie turned around and saw that he was being followed.

He picked up speed . . .

So the Superfairies flew faster . . .

And the magpie flew

Fast, Fast,
FASTER STILL . . .

Then the tricky bird vanished into a big snowy tree.

"Where is he now, Berry?" called Star.

"He must be hiding inside the tree," said Berry.

The Superfairies flew toward the tree. There was a hole in the middle of it.

"Look!" whispered Berry. "Something is sparkling in that hole!"

"You're right, Berry!" whispered Rose. "Let's be very quiet and fly toward it."

"There he is!" said Berry. She could see the magpie hiding inside with the crown in his clutches.

"I will do a dazzle," said Star.

"And then I will zoom in to get the crown!" said Silk.

Star prepared to dazzle.

Twinkle!

Dazzle!

Sparkle!

But the magpie quickly flew out of the hole. He soared into the snowy sky again.

"After him!" cried Rose.

Chapter 4

Back to the Sparkle Ball

As the Superfairies zoomed after the bird, the Snow Fairy appeared beside them in the air.

"I heard the bells and followed you," she said. "I will make sure he cannot fly any farther."

With that, she waved her wand and created a gentle blizzard of snow. The swirling snow made it impossible for the magpie to see where he was going.

The naughty bird stopped on the nearest branch for safety. The crown fell from his clutches.

Berry swooped in to catch the crown.

"Phew! Got it!" she cried.

"Hurrah!" cried the other Superfairies.

"Well done, Berry!" said Rose.

The Snow Fairy and the Superfairies checked that the magpie was okay.

"I'm sorry," said the magpie. "I can't help taking shiny things. I just love them so much!"

"But if they don't belong to you, then you shouldn't take them," Rose told him gently.

"I know! I will try my best not to!" promised the magpie. Then he flew off to find his nest.

Billy, Sonny, and Basil were delighted to see the crown returned safely.

"Phew," said Billy. "Thank you so much! That was all my fault. I'm so glad it turned out okay!"

"Same here," said Basil. "I was scared it was gone forever!"

"I wasn't nervous," said Sonny. "I knew the Superfairies would find it!"

Back at Icy Hollow, it was time for the crowning ceremony.

The band played a beautiful tune. A choir of animals sang to the Snow Fairy. She sat on her icy throne, shimmering with wisdom.

The music stopped as the Superfairies flew to the Snow Fairy.

"Are you ready and willing to be our Queen of Winter?" asked Rose.

"I am," said the Snow Fairy.

"Are you ready and willing to support us when we're in trouble?" asked Star.

"I am," said the Snow Fairy.

"Are you ready and willing to lead us toward spring?" asked Silk.

"I am," said the Snow Fairy.

"Are you ready and willing to celebrate the beauty of winter with us?" asked Berry.

"I am," said the Snow Fairy.

"Then," said Rose, placing the magnificent crown on the Snow Fairy's head, "I pronounce you the Queen of Winter!"

A huge cheer went up in Icy Hollow.

"Hush, everyone!" said Rose. "Let the new Winter Queen speak!"

"Thank you! Every one of you!" said the new Winter Queen. "After this party, I wish you all a beautiful sleep until spring! I will never let you down! And now, let's celebrate!"

"Hurrah!" cheered Billy, Sonny, and Basil. "All thanks to the Superfairies!"

"Let's do a line dance!" called Star, who loved to dance. "Come on, Dancer, help me!"

Susie and Violet followed the dance moves of Star and Dancer. Eventually the others joined in too, all holding hands.

"This is such fun!" said Susie. She could hardly dance as she was giggling so much.

"Billy, three steps *this* way!" called Martha. She gently pulled him in the right direction.

After the line dance, there was a waltz.

Finally, the Superfairies and the animals feasted together until everyone was exhausted. Then it was time for the Superfairies' song:

Fairies from the blossom tree,
Superskills galore have we.

Caring in this charming wood
For needy animals, as we should.

Twinkle, sparkle, dazzle, swish,
Tending animals as they wish.

And when a rescue's nicely done,
It's time to have some fairy fun.

Dancing, singing, twirling, glee,
All around our blossom tree!

Glossary

blizzard (BLIZ-erd) — a long, heavy snowstorm

borrow (BAWR-oh) — to take or receive something with the promise of returning it

ceremony (SER-uh-moh-nee) — a formal act or series of acts performed in some regular way according to fixed rules

crystal (KRIS-tl) — a quartz that is transparent or nearly so

relatives (REL-uh-tivz) — people connected by blood or marriage

swoop (swoop) — to dive or pounce suddenly like a hawk on its prey

Talk It Out

1. Talk about your favorite things in winter — playing in the snow, getting cozy inside, or going to fancy parties.

2. Why did the boys take the crown outside? Can you understand why they did this?

3. Did you feel sorry for Dancer and Cloud, pulling the caravan through the snow? Do you think animals struggle in winter?

Write It Down

1. Make a list of all the winter clothes you will need if going on a long journey through snow.

2. Design a beautiful invitation to the Sparkle Ball. You could draw snowdrops, snowflakes, the winter crown, the Superfairies, or the animals.

3. Write a letter from Rose to the Snow Fairy, thanking her for such a lovely party.

All About Fairies

The legend of fairies is as old as time.
Fairy tales tell stories of fairy magic.
According to legend, fairies are so small
and delicate, and fly so fast, that they might
actually be all around us, but just very
hard to see. Fairies, supposedly, only reveal
themselves to believers.

Fairies often dance in circles at sunrise
and sunset. They love to play in woodlands
among wildflowers. If you sing gently to
them, they may appear.

Here are some of the world's most famous
fairies:

The Flower Fairies

Artist Cicely Mary Barker painted a
range of pretty flower fairies and published
eight volumes of flower fairy art beginning in
1923. The link between fairies and flowers is
very strong.

The Tooth Fairy

She visits us during the night to leave a coin when we lose our baby teeth. Although it is very hard to catch sight of the Tooth Fairy, children are always happy when she visits.

Fake Fairies

In 1917, cousins Elsie Wright and Frances Griffiths said they photographed fairies in their garden. They later admitted that most were fakes — but Frances claimed that one was genuine.

Which Superfairy Are You?

1. What gift would you most like in winter?
   - A)   a cozy scarf
   - B)   a jar of cookies
   - C)   a sparkly necklace
   - D)   a storybook

2. What is your favorite game?
   - A)   hopscotch
   - B)   Mother May I ?
   - C)   hide-and-go-seek
   - D)   tag

3. Which is your least-favorite school subject?
   - A)   art
   - B)   English
   - C)   math
   - D)   gym

4. What color would you wear to a winter ball?
   - A)   red
   - B)   purple
   - C)   gold
   - D)   pink

5. If you had a winter wish, you would . . .
   - A)   hold a world-wide party!
   - B)   make jewelry from icicles.
   - C)   dance in the snow.
   - D)   heal everyone who is hurting.

6. You enjoy movies about . . .
   - A)   adventures
   - B)   animals
   - C)   dancing
   - D)   fairies

7. Your favorite tree is . . .
   - A)   oak
   - B)   fir
   - C)   willow
   - D)   cherry blossom

8. The treat you would make for a winter party is . . .
   - A)   chocolate cake
   - B)   apple pie
   - C)   cheesecake
   - D)   white-chocolate mousse

Mostly A —You are like Berry! You are helpful, sweet, and full of good ideas.

Mostly B —You are like Silk! You are exciting, brave, and adventurous.

Mostly C —You are like Star! You are cheerful, funny, dazzling, and bold.

Mostly D —You are like Rose! You are gentle, sensible, kind, and caring.

About the Author

Janey Louise Jones has been a published author for ten years. Her Princess Poppy series is an international bestselling brand, with books translated into ten languages, including Hebrew and Mandarin. Janey is a graduate of Edinburgh University and lives in Edinburgh, Scotland, with her three sons. She loves fairies, princesses, beaches, and woodlands.

About the Illustrator

Jennie Poh was born in England and grew up in Malaysia (in the jungle). At the age of ten she moved back to England and trained as a ballet dancer. She studied fine art at Surrey Institute of Art & Design as well as fashion illustration at Central Saint Martins. Jennie loves the countryside, animals, tea, and reading. She lives in Woking, England, with her husband and two wonderful daughters.